LONE WOLF

SARAH KURPIEL

GREENWILLOW BOOKS, *an Imprint of HarperCollins Publishers*

Lone Wolf
Copyright © 2020 by Sarah Kurpiel
All rights reserved. Manufactured in China.
For information address HarperCollins Children's Books,
a division of HarperCollins Publishers, 195 Broadway, New York, NY 10007.
www.harpercollinschildrens.com

The illustrations were created digitally.
The text type is Directors Cut Pro.

Library of Congress Cataloging-in-Publication Data
Names: Kurpiel, Sarah, author, illustrator.
Title: Lone wolf / written and illustrated by Sarah Kurpiel.
Description: First edition. | New York, NY : Greenwillow Books, an imprint of
HarperCollins Publishers, [2020] | Summary: So many people think Maple is
a wolf that she starts to believe them, but after exploring the world
outside her home, she returns to her pack—the Parker family.
Identifiers: LCCN 2019016309 | ISBN 9780062943828 (hardcover)
Subjects: | CYAC: Dogs—Fiction. | Identity—Fiction.
Classification: LCC PZ7.1.K87 Lon 2020 | DDC [E]—dc23 LC record available at
https://lccn.loc.gov/2019016309
20 21 22 23 24 SCP 10 9 8 7 6 5 4 3 2 1
First Edition
Greenwillow Books

For Mom,
Dad, & Mikayla

Maple loved
being the Parker
family dog.

Every day, she played
tug-of-war with Jax,

read with Avery
on the couch,

and tricked Mom
and Dad into giving
her extra treats

and taking her on e x t r a - l o n g walks.

But on her walks, people would say . . .

"Dude, that dog looks like a wolf."

"WOLF!
WOLF!
WOLF!"

"Are you sure she's
not part wolf?"

The Parkers tried to explain that
Maple was not, in fact, a wolf.

Eventually, though, even
Maple had her doubts.

She looked more like a wolf
than all the other dogs.

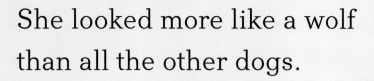

She could hunt like a wolf,

howl like a wolf,

and dig like a wolf, too.

Maybe she *was* a wolf. And wolves belong
in the wild, not in houses or dog parks,
not on couches or sidewalks.

So one day, when the fence was open
just an inch for just a moment . . .

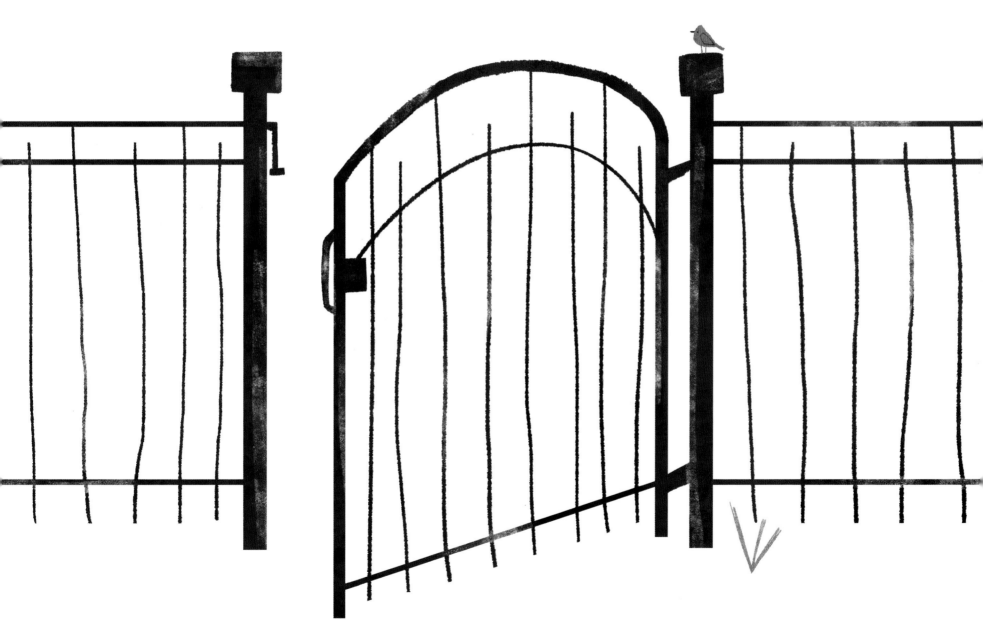

an inch and a moment
was all it took.

But out in the wild,
the ground was tougher
than Dad's flower garden,

squirrels were harder
to hunt than Avery's flip-flops,

and the perfect
tug-of-war stick

was just a stick
if Jax wasn't on the other end.

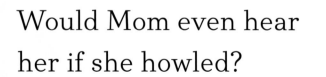

Would Mom even hear
her if she howled?

Maple didn't want to be
a wolf anymore.

Then she remembered
it was time for her evening walk.
Maple *never* missed a walk.
So she followed her nose out of the woods

and through the neighborhood.
And on her walk she found . . .

her pack!

Some people still thought Maple was a wolf.

But Maple knew who she really was.

She was a Parker.
And she was right . . .

where she belonged.